Elephant in the Kitchen

This book is dedicated to
Lachlan Rennie and Danny Robinson,
the first of the second generation
to hear the story.

Elephant in the Kitchen

by Winsome Smith

Illustrated by Stephen Axelsen

Ashton Scholastic

Sydney Auckland New York Toronto London

National Library of Australia
Cataloguing-in-Publication data

Smith, Winsome Gloria.
Elephant in the kitchen.
For children
ISBN 0 86896 135 3
1. Axelsen, Stephen, illus.
2. Title.

A823'.3

First published in 1980 by Ashton Scholastic, P.O. Box
579, Gosford, N.S.W.

Printed by Hedges & Bell, Sutton Road, Maryborough,
Victoria 3465

6 5 4 3 2 1   0 1 2 3/8

Contents

Chapter 1   Angry Beginnings   7
2   The Last Act   11
3   Where's Cato?   17
4   Elephant in Danger   20
5   Arriving home   26
6   Hay in the Kitchen?   30
7   Elephant in the Newspaper   35
8   Cato Follows His Trunk   41
9   This Place is Unsafe   46
10   John Darcy's Brilliant Idea   49
11   In the Newspaper Again   55
12   The Discovery of Peanut Butter   60
13   The Meeting of Old Friends   64
14   Animal Tracks   69
15   If Ye Be Angry Enough . . .   74
16   Meeting a Millionaire   80
17   Sam's Big Decision   85
18   Sam's Party   92
19   Danger in the Kitchen   94
20   The Uninvited Guest   99
21   The Magician Who Changed Himself   107

ANGRY BEGINNINGS

"I want *my* name at the top of the poster!" raged Le Vram the magician, and at each word his red face grew even redder.

"But you are *not* the star of this circus!" insisted Mr Borrill, the circus owner, thumping the table with a fat fist.

Mr Borrill and Le Vram had to stand so close together in Mr Borrill's caravan that their noses were almost touching. Every time Mr Borrill thumped on the table, the caravan jumped and shook.

"This poster is an insult!" shouted the magician, his eyes flashing. He grabbed a poster from the table and waved it in Mr Borrill's face.

Ta-ra-ta-tum-BOOM-BOOM blared the brass band in the big top nearby. The afternoon circus performance was in progress, but the music could not drown out the performance that was going on inside the caravan.

"I suppose you think," Le Vram continued, "that that elephant, Cato, is the star of the circus."

"Cato *is* the star," replied Mr Borrill. "You're not—not by any means. It was I who arranged for Sam Fleming, the artist, to design the poster this way."

Mr Borrill, his tartan waistcoat and gold watch-chain stretched tight across his expansive middle, snatched the poster from Le Vram and jabbed at it with a chubby finger.

"Come to Borrill's Circus," he read loudly and clearly, "Starring Cato, the Elephant of Amazing Talent."

Then he said to Le Vram: "In my circus I've got trapeze artists, acrobats, performing horses, dogs and lions. I've got clowns, tumblers, and a man who eats fire. They're all great performers, but the main attraction is Cato, the elephant. He's the star. I would put *all* my performers on that poster before the name of a second-rate magician."

"Call me second-rate, would you?" fumed Le Vram. His face was now turning from red to white.

"Of course," replied Mr Borrill. "Remember the time you got a boy from the audience to help you, and he was better at magic than you were? Remember the time you went to pull a rabbit out of a hat and the rabbit wasn't there? Remember the time you tried to make a lady disappear, but you fused the lights and the whole circus was plunged into darkness? Your magic doesn't work! Magicians don't belong in circuses anyway. I only gave you the job because I felt sorry for you."

Da-da-da-BOOM-da-da came from the tent, then the music stopped. There came a sound like lots of leaves being flapped together by a strong wind.

"Hear that sound?" asked Mr Borrill. "Do you hear that sound? That's applause. That is the sound of many people clapping, and if you listen carefully, you will also hear the laughter of children who are enjoying my circus and, if I'm not mistaken, clapping for more of Cato. And that is why Cato is the star of my show. He gets applause. You don't."

"I'll ruin you for this," snarled Le Vram. He was no longer shouting, but had grown quiet. "The Great Le Vram called second-rate? I'm leaving, but you'll pay for this outrage. I'll show you whether or not my magic works."

Le Vram stormed out of the caravan, banging the door so hard that the caravan shook and Mr Borrill's bright new posters scattered across the floor.

The angry magician stamped down the wooden steps and strode towards his own caravan.

"Thunderation!" he raged. "Thunderation. Hurricane, pestilence and devastation!" He spat each word emphatically.

When he came to his own caravan he flopped onto the steps and waved his arms about angrily, muttering to himself.

"Rabbits out of hats . . . disappearing ladies . . . Nonsense for amateurs, all of it! That foolishness is not for me, the Great Le Vram. No—evil is my specialty—evil and revenge. Evil spells that really work. They *work,* I say! That is, unless there is too much . . .," he hesitated to say the dreadful word, "too much . . . goodness—around. Yes, too much goodness, kindness, thoughtfulness and generosity. Too much of that is the only thing that can spoil my magic."

He stopped as he heard more laughter and cheering from inside the big top.

"Little children laughing! Thunder and plague! Fancy me, with all my ancient and dreadful skills, being reduced to working in a circus. Making little children laugh. Bah!"

Suddenly feeling old and tired, he crumpled up on the

caravan steps. "It's too much for me. I'll retire, that's what I'll do. I'll retire from working as a magician. I can retire to my house in the mountains. But first of all—REVENGE!"

He stood up and flung his arms wide. "Revenge! I'll ruin Borrill and his circus. People who upset magicians deserve to be ruined. I'll show them. They can't treat *me* like this."

CHAPTER 2

THE LAST ACT

The audience inside the big top knew nothing of what had happened in Mr Borrill's caravan. Everyone was totally engrossed in what was taking place in the sawdust ring. In one of the front seats, John Darcy straightened his glasses so he could see the last part of the elephant act even more clearly.

Because his uncle, Sam Fleming, had painted posters for the circus, John Darcy had been given a free seat and had attended every performance since the circus came to town.

As he looked around, he decided that the elephant act was definitely everyone's favourite. The children sitting nearby applauded wildly as Cato stole a cap from a little boy's head, and waltzed around the ring waving the cap in the air. A clown, pretending to chase one of the elephants, tripped on a rope and rolled over in somersaults.

John Darcy had once heard Cato's trainer say that sometimes Cato was just too lazy to do his tricks properly in the ring, even though he knew how to do them very well.

This seemed to be true, because when he was in the ring Cato made one mistake after another.

John Darcy had noticed that whenever the children laughed at a mistake, Cato made another, and another, until the whole of the audience was in an uproar. If, however, nobody laughed at a mistake, Cato performed perfectly, never taking a wrong step and obeying every command. It occurred to John Darcy that Cato must be a particularly clever elephant. He knew exactly when to perform correctly and when not to.

In their little enclosure beside the ring, the musicians puffed into brass instruments, twiddled with keys, and tapped with drumsticks as Cato's act drew to a close.

"Encore!" shouted someone in a back seat.

Dah-da-da-BOOM-da-da, played the band. It was the signal for Cato to return and perform extra tricks.

This was the part where Cato let his head go and did whatever he felt like. The audience cheered as he lifted a surprised circus worker off his feet, and then stole a bag of peanuts from the peanut seller.

When Cato's act was finally over, he was led to the main exit. There he stood while the last act, the trapeze performance, was in progress. When the circus was over, Cato would nod goodbye to the people as they walked past him.

Across the ring from John Darcy, a tall, thin man with a bushy black beard sat on a high wooden stool. He was Sam Fleming, the artist. He balanced a sketch pad on his lap as he made quick drawings of everything he saw. Every time he finished a page, he would tear it off the pad and start a fresh one. He worked quickly; there was so much in the ring that he wanted to draw.

Beside Sam stood his friend, Stella Borrill, the circus owner's daughter. She had known circus life ever since she was a little girl. She had often performed on the tightrope, but now she preferred to help manage the circus and look after the money side of things.

"You've drawn the elephants beautifully," she said to Sam, "especially Cato."

"I wanted to show how graceful and clever they are," Sam replied.

"That's just what you've done," said Stella.

She picked up some loose pages from the ground and looked at them again. Although these were only quick sketches, Stella could see the kind of paintings they were going to be. Sam's trapeze fliers seemed about to swing right off the page. His horses leaped and pranced so that their hooves seemed to twinkle. The sketch of the balancing act showed every straining muscle and such hairsbreadth balance that Stella held her breath and winced.

"This is the circus, Sam," she said as she put the drawings back on the ground. "You've taken the circus and put it onto paper."

Sam grinned back at her.

The band changed from catchy dance music to a marching tune. The circus was over. The audience sat still in their seats for a minute, then began to struggle slowly towards the exits. John Darcy left his seat and, stepping gingerly over the stakes and ropes, made his way across the ring to meet Sam.

Over at the main exit, Cato nodded his head and swayed his trunk as the people filed past him. This was the part of the show he liked best. His bright little eyes sparkled as the children patted him. They gave him peanuts or potato crisps or biscuits, and these he took delicately in his trunk and put into his mouth.

Near the main ring, John Darcy said hello to Stella, then turned to Sam. He adjusted his glasses and peered at Sam's last drawing.

"Hmm, not bad, Sam," he remarked approvingly. Then he remembered something. "Mum told me to remind you about tonight."

"What about tonight?" asked Sam, adding a few lines to his sketch.

"You're coming to our house for dinner," John Darcy told him. "Mum said that if I don't remind you, you'll forget."

Sam looked up from his drawing and grinned. "I can never convince my sister that I really do eat very well. She thinks I can't look after myself properly."

When the tent was almost empty, the circus workers hurried to clean up so that the tent would be ready for the evening performance. Sam began packing his equipment away in the battered old suitcase beside him on the ground. He put his collection of sketches into a flat cardboard folder and tied it with tape.

It was at that moment that a rushing, swishing sound was heard. Le Vram the magician, with a face as angry as a thundercloud, stormed into the big top. He wore the outfit he had worn for his act: a scarlet cloak (a little crushed), black patent shoes (a little dusty), a top hat (a little lopsided), a black suit (rather threadbare), and a shirt that had once been white.

His heavy black brows were drawn together with anger.

Before Sam, John Darcy and Stella could make a move, Le Vram pushed past them, knocking Sam's case to the ground and scattering his pencils and pads in the sawdust. He continued across the ring and charged out the main exit.

"Hey, watch what you're doing!" yelled Sam after the magician's fleeing figure.

Alarmed and puzzled, Sam and his friends knelt down and began to pick up the things that had been scattered. They shook the sawdust out of the sketch pads and gathered up the pencils.

Suddenly they heard a startled cry from the exit. They looked up quickly and saw the elephant trainer waving his arms in the air, with a look of disbelief on his face.

"Call Mr Borrill!" the trainer shouted. "Get the police! Do something, anything! Cato has disappeared!"

CHAPTER 3

WHERE'S CATO?

It was a flustered and breathless clown who knocked on the door of Mr Borrill's caravan. Mr Borrill, still angry after the argument with Le Vram, opened the door.

"What do you want?" he snapped.

"Cato has disappeared. You'd better come to the big top straight away," the clown blurted out. The wide grin painted on his face did not match the worried frown he also wore.

"Ridiculous!" scoffed Mr Borrill. "It's impossible to lose an elephant. What on earth are you people doing over there? Go back and find him."

He banged the door shut, then immediately opened it again.

"I'm sorry," he said, "I'm not usually like this. It's just that I've had a rather upsetting afternoon. Come on, we'll look into this."

Together the two hurried across the grass to the big top.

"It looks like a case for the police," the clown said.

"You're worrying unnecessarily," Mr Borrill replied as he lifted the curtain and entered the big top. "Elephants don't disappear. Let's not lose our heads."

Mystified circus people wandered around the big top, calling "Cato, Cato."

It was John Darcy who announced: "This is silly. There is absolutely nowhere for an elephant to hide in here. He must be outside among the caravans and cages."

As they searched, the feelings of the circus people changed from disbelief to worry, then finally to panic. Clowns, acrobats and jugglers, still in their costumes, rushed hither and thither, bumping into each other, and calling Cato's name.

The two young policemen who had been called were just as mystified as everyone else. Such a thing had never happened in the town before. They had dealt with robberies and lost children, but neither of them had ever had to search for a lost elephant.

They had asked everyone a lot of questions and written things down in their notebooks, but found not one clue. An hour later, Mr Borrill took out his handkerchief and, looking as though he might cry, said to Stella, "This is the worst thing that has ever happened to me. If Cato isn't found our circus will be ruined."

"We shouldn't look on the gloomy side, Father," said Stella comfortingly. "You said yourself that elephants don't get lost. We ought to be getting ready for the evening performance anyway. The circus can go on, even without Cato."

"Nonsense, my dear. The time has come for us to face facts. All that laughing and cheering, and all those happy faces—it's only because of one performer . . . Cato. He is a real actor, that elephant. He even makes his mistakes look funny."

Blowing his nose, he said, "The children love Cato. And it is children's joy that *makes* a circus."

CHAPTER 4

ELEPHANT IN DANGER

Cato was just as puzzled about what had happened as everyone else. He had been standing by the door of the big top, the way he always did, nodding and swaying, his eyes twinkling as the crowd shuffled past him.

After the last of the children had patted him and he had eaten the last peanut, he stood waiting patiently for his trainer. He was looking forward to a nice meal of hay and a good rest before the evening performance. The workmen were busy, tightening ropes and sweeping up rubbish.

When Le Vram rushed into the tent, Cato did not take very much notice. It was easy to see that the magician was in a temper about something, but there was nothing very unusual about that. Cato simply went on thinking about things like hay and peanuts and the way the children had clapped for him.

Le Vram stormed across the sawdust ring, then stopped in front of Cato. He reached up and let his hand rest on the elephant's trunk. Although the magician had never done this before, Cato hardly gave it a thought. He had been patted so often that afternoon that one more hand on his trunk made no difference. Le Vram left the tent.

Unusual feelings swept over Cato. One minute he was standing in the circus tent, and the next minute he was surrounded by a forest of grass—so tall that it was over his head.

Feeling stranger by the second, he shook his legs one by one. First he shook his right front leg, then his left front leg, then he shook his right hind leg. It was when he shook his left hind leg that he realised that something was definitely wrong. The chain he always wore around his ankle was missing.

I'm in the jungle, Cato thought. It's magic. I've been taken from the circus, and transported back to the jungle.

Tall grass waved about him. His feet sank into a tangle of roots beneath him. He began to push through the grassy forest, but soon his way was blocked by a pile of rocks. Puzzled, he stopped for a moment to think. Should he go to the left or to the right? Where did he want to get to anyway? How ever was he going to get back to the circus? If he kept walking, he might soon come to a river or a road, or even a herd of elephants. That would be nice. It was rather lonely in this strange jungle.

Walking closer to the rocks, he realised they were red and green and gold—and almost transparent. The rocks sparkled with a fine coating of silvery dust. More of this dust was scattered on the ground and it glittered amongst the jungle grass.

Cautiously, Cato stepped around the bright boulders—and there, behind them, was the entrance to a cave. It was a tall, narrow entrance, rising above the ground. Coloured boulders were scattered about the entrance.

Cato put out his trunk, and waved it around inside the cave before he ventured in. There was a sweet smell; not unpleasant and strangely familiar.

Suddenly the sky darkened. A shadow fell across the earth. The ground shook. Thunder rolled above. The noise of a gigantic storm roared about him. Cato crouched in the entrance of the cave waiting for the rain to start. Instead of rain, an enormous object crashed into the long grass nearby.

A caravan? wondered Cato, extremely puzzled. It was as big as a caravan, but was a shabby brown, not brightly painted like the circus caravans. The tyres at the back were not round, but were long and thick and straight, just like the sole of a . . .

Cato shuddered. He was looking at a giant boot.

But why would such a gigantic boot be here in the jungle? Cato took a step backwards into the cave. As he did so, he bumped against a red boulder. It rolled gently to one side, and Cato saw that it was not hard—it was soft.

Then he realised why that sweet smell was familiar. Those rocks were jubes, coated with sugar, and this cave was the jube packet dropped by some careless person. He was not in the jungle after all, but still at the circus!

Cato looked up and saw that the boot was attached to an enormous leg. A short distance away was another leg, and both were attached to a man whose head was so far up that Cato could barely see it. The head turned and Cato could see that it was his trainer.

Cato knew then that something strange had indeed

happened. He had not been transported to another place. He was still here in the circus—but he had shrunk! He was now as tiny as a mouse.

Still the thunder roared above him, but Cato now recognised it as voices—worried, human voices.

"Call Mr Borrill! Get the police! Do something, anything! Cato has disappeared!"

"Cato, where are you?"

"Cato, Cato."

The tiny elephant felt his heart pounding. Never before had he been in danger, and never had he felt so afraid. He knew that he could be crushed at any moment by rushing boots. Where could he hide?

Peering up through the grass, he could see the doorway of the big top; a doorway through which, any moment, people might run. Giant people. A cardboard jube-box could not protect him from them.

Not far away there should be a curtain. Cato turned around. Yes, there it was, right behind him. He lifted it with his trunk and struggled under. From memory he knew that he should now be under the seats.

He looked up again. Sure enough, the planks of the seats rose in steps above him, making many ceilings. Here at least he would be safe for a while.

But not for long. He heard gusts of wind, as a panting, slobbering dog sniffed at the ground near him. Creaking wheels churned past as cages were rolled around. Hurrying feet thundered by. The circus had once been home and safety and friends—but now it meant only danger.

Among the medley of sounds, Cato heard Mr Borrill's worried voice. "He can't be lost. We'll search everywhere. Look behind the caravans, behind the trucks, among the small cages. Look behind every curtain in this tent. Cato must be found!"

Now there was even more danger, as people began to move things around. At any moment a heavy box, crate or plank could land right on top of him. Everyone was looking for a large elephant, not a tiny one.

On the ground, nearby, Cato noticed an open suitcase. It was as big as a house and it lay tipped sideways against some ropes. There were enormous sheets of paper and massive pencils spilling out. It would be much safer there, away from those great, hurrying boots. When the noise and shouting had died down a little, he hurried towards the suitcase. A bundle of ropes beside it made a kind of ramp, so he was able to walk up to the edge. Carefully he stepped from the rope onto some sheets of paper and, with a gentle thud, slid down among pencils, erasers, sketch pads and drawing charcoal.

He snuggled comfortably among sheets of drawings, and listened to the sounds around him. Voices shouted, boots thudded, dogs barked. In the distance, lions roared. He reached out with his trunk and pulled a sheet of paper over himself. Here he felt safe. Here he stayed for a long time, while everyone from the circus searched for him.

Suddenly there was a sharp bang above him and everything became dark. The lid of the suitcase had been closed. Cato was thrown upside down as the case was lifted into the air. The case swayed sickeningly as Sam Fleming, without knowing it, carried Cato away from the circus.

CHAPTER 5

ARRIVING HOME

"It's an astonishing thing,'
remarked John Darcy a short while later, as he and Sam
walked through town on their way home. "I thought it
would be impossible to lose an elephant."

"Just look at that sunset," murmured Sam absently. In
one hand he carried his case which swung as he strode
along. His big folder of drawings was tucked under the
other arm.

"I know people lose things—but an elephant!" John
Darcy continued.

"I could paint that in shades of gold and apricot," said
Sam.

"I mean, they're so big they're easy to see," said John
Darcy.

"Of course they are," replied Sam. "They fill the whole
western sky."

"Elephants in the sky?" exclaimed John Darcy.

"No, sunsets," said Sam, looking down at his young nephew in surprise.

"The trouble with you, Sam, is that you can't think of anything except drawing and painting," John Darcy scolded. "I wasn't talking about sunsets. I was talking about losing things."

"Oh, of course," Sam replied. "That's not unusual. I lose lots of things."

"Don't I know it!" John Darcy sounded exasperated. "I help you search for things all the time. But you lose things like pencils, socks, cash, tubes of paint. You've never lost an elephant, have you?"

Sam looked thoughtful and said with a smile, "No. No, I must admit, I've never lost an elephant."

It was becoming dark and lights were being flicked on in the windows of the houses in the little town.

Sam Fleming, with his baggy old jumper, his ragged jeans, and his floppy way of walking, looked just like a puppet on a string. His marvellous black beard sprouted like a spray of leaves at the top of a tall, slender tree.

John Darcy was eleven. Where Sam had untidy and disorganised ways, John Darcy was neat and orderly. He wore black-rimmed glasses with thick lenses that made him look something like a thin, neatly-dressed owl.

In his class at school there were four other boys named John—John Roberts, John Smith, John Hebblewhite and John Barker. The teacher always called the boys by their full names so that there was no confusion. John Darcy was hardly ever called just plain 'John'. Even his mother, Mrs Annie Darcy, called him John Darcy most of the time.

Although they lived in a very small town, the walk home took a long time because Sam had so many friends. He stopped to chat with Nick at the fish shop and the man at the fruit shop. He said hello to everyone he passed.

By the time they arrived home it was dark, and the street lights were sending out a pale glow. The picture theatre across the road was open, but people had not yet begun to line up at the ticket box.

John Darcy lived with his widowed mother in a cottage, neat and pretty enough to be a picture on a calendar. Sam Fleming lived in a ramshackle studio he had built for himself in the Darcy's back yard.

Mrs Darcy often tried to get Sam, her brother, to move into her spare room, but he always refused.

"There might be room for me in that spare room, Annie," he would tell her, "but where would I put my paints, my paintings and drawings? Anyway, you like things tidy. You couldn't stand having someone as messy as me in your house."

Mrs Darcy knew he was right, but she still worried. In her opinion Sam could not look after himself. Because of this she often made him puddings and soup, and she tried to get him to eat fruit. She darned his socks (when they could be found), and she sometimes insisted on him having dinner with John Darcy and her. Mostly, though, she left him to do his painting in the happy mess of his tumbledown home.

"My goodness, you two are late!" she exclaimed when she saw John Darcy and Sam. "I got back from the Childrens Home Committee meeting ages ago. There's a steak-and-kidney pie in the oven. I've got some important news for you, Sam. Come on now."

"And we've got news for you, Mum," said John Darcy. "There's an elephant missing from the circus and . . ."

"Yes, dear," interrupted his mother. "Tell me all about it while we have tea. Sam, where are you off to?"

Sam, who was dashing across the yard, called, "Just a minute, Annie. Some idiot knocked my bag over at the circus. I'll just put it inside and check that the sketches are still okay."

"Well, don't be too long," said his sister.

Sam rushed into his studio, dropped his folder on the floor, and flung his suitcase onto the kitchen bench.

"Now, let's hope everything's all right," he muttered. He switched on the light and, opening the suitcase, picked up the top sheet of paper.

"Botheration! This has got dirt on it. I'll have to throw it out." He crumpled up the sheet and flung it to one side. He bent over the case again. "Now, let's see. That charcoal stick, did it fall out?"

He reached into the case.

"Sam!" came John Darcy's voice from the doorway. "Sam, Mum's waiting—and I'm starving. Come and have tea now."

"Well, all right. I can fix this up later," said Sam.

Leaving the suitcase open on the kitchen bench, he hurried out.

CHAPTER 6

HAY IN THE KITCHEN?

Cato listened. Everything was quiet in the studio—except for the *plop, plop, plop* of a dripping tap. When he was sure no one was likely to see him, he pushed aside some papers and stood up. Like all elephants, he hated being carried around in a suitcase, and he felt stiff and bruised and cranky. He wanted to be back at the circus having a nice meal of hay and perhaps a few apples.

Cato clambered onto the piled-up sketches, then stepped down onto the suitcase's open lid. He walked down the lid, climbed over the edge, and found himself, if not on firm ground, at least on a firm kitchen bench. He stretched his aching limbs and had a good look around.

So this is what the inside of a house looks like, he thought to himself.

Sam's home had only two rooms—a studio where he worked and slept, and a kitchen where he cooked. A doorway separated the two rooms, and through this Cato could see into the studio beyond.

He saw a big, untidy, muddled work-room—obviously a room where someone loved to dabble in paint. In the middle of the studio there stood a large table that Sam called his 'workbench'. On this there was a jumble of paint tubes, jars of brushes, old paint-covered rags, sticks of charcoal, and unfinished sketches.

Sam's clothes, coffee mugs and paintings were scattered from one end of the studio to the other in a wonderful confusion. Even Sam's bed, against the wall at the far end, had a pile of pictures stacked on it.

From the kitchen bench, Cato could just see a window along the side wall of the studio. It was almost as big as the wall, and looked out across the street to the picture theatre over the road.

Sam's kitchen was a beautiful, happy mess. In the middle there was a cupboard with a bench on top, and it was here that Cato was standing. Beside this bench was a sink, and on the other side of the sink stood an old-fashioned dresser.

It was a rickety, battered old dresser—so old that it leaned to one side. It was the type that had a tall plate rack above and a cupboard below. The rack was filled with plates and cups. Beneath that, the top of the dresser cupboard was littered with household and artistic articles of every possible kind.

Nearly every letter that Sam had ever received had been thrown unopened onto the dresser top. Sam hated opening letters because they were usually bills. A leather wallet lay open, with money and papers falling out. There were saucepans, a packet of cheese, a carton of eggs, and one brown suede shoe. A grey woollen jumper lay among some tubes of paint, with one of its sleeves hanging lazily down over a deep dresser drawer. The old dresser top was worn. In one place the wood had split open, leaving a large, gaping hole.

Although Sam always washed his dishes, he hardly ever put them away. Cups, plates, mugs and cutlery littered the bench where Cato stood. There were also packets of biscuits, bread on a breadboard, apples in a dish, a coffee mug full of paintbrushes, and pencils in a jam jar.

Again Cato heard the *plop, plop, plop* of water, and discovered that it was the tap over the sink that was dripping. Feeling very thirsty after such an eventful afternoon, he started to make his way towards the tap.

Sam's wire dish-drainer stood in the sink, leaning against the side. It made a handy ladder down into the stainless steel depths of the sink, so Cato clambered unsteadily down.

Little puddles of water lay here and there on the uneven bottom of the cold steel sink. Cato took a long, refreshing drink. Then he stood directly under the dripping tap and let the drops of water run over him. Water trickled over his head and neck and back, and settled in little pools around his feet. How cool and clean and fresh it felt—almost as good as being under the hose.

Then he remembered that Sam might soon come back, and perhaps the sight of an elephant in the kitchen would startle him. Reluctantly, he climbed up the dish drainer again.

Listening carefully for Sam, he explored the kitchen cupboards, hoping to find something to eat. He could hardly expect to find any hay in the kitchen, but there just might be something tasty.

On the dresser, behind the suede shoe, he came across a half-empty tin of spaghetti. Dipping in his trunk, he pulled out a short, soft, juicy rope. Not bad, he thought as he tasted it, not bad at all.

Just as he was finishing the last of the spaghetti, something caught his attention. Had he heard a noise? Yes, the sound of footsteps. He remembered he was not his normal size. He also remembered those colossal boots that nearly trampled him at the circus. His first thought now was safety, so he looked around for a place to hide.

The footsteps came closer. Cato took a few short steps, slipped and lurched forward. Air rushed past his ears as he fell. He heard a gentle rustling and crumpling sound as he rolled over onto his feet and discovered he was on a cushion of soft tracing paper. He looked around. He had fallen straight through that hole in the dresser and was now inside the deep drawer.

The studio door opened with a creak, then closed again. Cato hid in the paper and listened.

CHAPTER 7

ELEPHANT IN THE NEWSPAPER

"Yes, that's what the man from the town council told me, Sam," said Mrs Darcy as the three of them entered Sam's kitchen. "He believes this place is unsafe and has to be pulled down before it falls on top of someone."

"Annie, did you explain to him that this is my home? I built it myself." Sam sounded annoyed.

"Of course I did," she answered. "I thought the man was very rude telling me my backyard was an eyesore. It didn't make any difference though. He said that if you don't pull it down, the council will come and pull it down for you."

John Darcy leaned against the sink and looked around. Yes, the building was an eyesore. Although Sam was a very good artist, he was not a very good builder. The place served quite well as a studio, but Sam was usually too busy to notice that the roof leaked and there were cracks in the walls.

John Darcy's eye was caught by a row of wet dots going from the sink to the dresser. He leaned a little closer. I wonder how that happened, he thought.

A soft, rustling sound came from the dresser drawer. Mice, thought John Darcy.

While his mother and Sam talked, he moved over to the dresser. The same round, wet dots were on top of it. They certainly aren't mouse tracks, John Darcy mused, but nothing else would be small enough to be rustling around in a dresser drawer.

He put his hand on the drawer handle and pulled. Nothing happened. The drawer was stuck. The dresser leaned so far to one side that, although the cupboard doors at the bottom hung open, the drawer was jammed shut.

He pulled the handle again. He rattled it. The drawer stayed closed.

"Sam, do you know you've got mice?" he asked, turning around.

"Mice!" exclaimed Mrs Darcy, before Sam could answer. "I wouldn't be surprised if you had whole families of mice in those cupboards, Sam. Have you ever cleaned them out?"

"Of course I have," Sam replied. "I cleaned them out only three years ago. I can guarantee there are no mice there."

Mrs Darcy continued, "Just look at those gaps in the roof. Sam dear, I think the council is right. You'll have to move into the house and pull this dangerous place down, before you have a nasty accident."

"That's impossible," said Sam. "It's a kind offer, but there isn't room for me and all my equipment in your house."

"Then you'll have to buy or rent another place," said his sister.

"Also impossible," declared Sam, as he picked up his folder from the floor and began sorting his sketches. "You know I haven't got any money. Just about every cent I earn is spent on art materials."

"Sam, that's ridiculous! You just don't look after your money. You should have thousands saved up. Haven't you got a bank account?"

"I never have any money to put into the bank," Sam replied. He held up one of his circus sketches. "Just look at this. Isn't she beautiful?"

It was Stella, poised on a tightrope; a picture of perfect balance. It was as though the artist had been on the same level as Stella, because behind her, and below, was the dizzy mass of upturned faces in the crowd. The whole background was blurred, just as Stella, glancing down, might have seen it.

Mrs Darcy, who admired her brother's work a great deal, took the picture in her hands to get a closer look.

"Yes, it is very well done, Sam," she said. "I don't know how it is that you haven't got plenty of money when you do work as good as this."

* * *

The next morning John Darcy, neatly dressed in his school uniform, rushed into the studio waving a newspaper.

"Just look at this, Sam."

Sam was standing at an easel working, while a cup of coffee got cold on the floor beside him.

"Something about Cato?" he asked.

"A lot about Cato," said John Darcy, handing him the paper.

Sam looked at the page and read aloud:

Elephant Lost

Strange Disappearance of Circus Favourite

Local police are baffled by the mysterious disappearance of an elephant from Borrill's Circus late yesterday afternoon . . .

"So he hasn't been found yet," he remarked, glancing up.

"No," answered John Darcy. "There's a lot more in the newspaper story—and look above the story. There's a photograph of Mr Borrill and Stella."

"So there is. And under that it says: 'Mr Borrill told reporters that without Cato his circus would be ruined'."

"Well, I'm off to school," said John Darcy. "I've got to get there early to change my library books. Mum said to remind you that the man from the council is coming to see you today. And keep an eye out for that elephant."

* * *

Sam Fleming and John Darcy were not the only ones to show great interest in the headlines that morning.

In an old brick cottage surrounded by an overgrown

garden, in a town in the mountains, a surprised Le Vram read the news about Cato over and over again.

He looked rather different from the jealous magician who had quarrelled with Mr Borrill. He wore a crumpled, checked dressing-gown and old slippers with holes at the toes. His lopsided top hat hung on a hook near the front door, and his crushed, scarlet cloak lay in a heap on the floor, just where he had left it. He ate his morning cereal from a chipped plate. Le Vram looked like a man who no longer cared about anything.

As he read the item in the newspaper, little lines began to appear at the corners of his eyes. It was the beginning of a smile.

"Strange Disappearance," he read aloud for the fifth time. A little twinkle came into his eyes. "I did it," he said in a hushed voice. His mouth twitched into a grin. "I did it," he said again. "I made something disappear." His mouth curled into a smile. He leapt to his feet. "I did it!" he shouted. He laughed out loud and skipped about. "At last I've done the Ancient Disappearing Trick. I made something disappear."

He ran to a bookcase near the window and began to rummage among the old, leather-covered volumes. As he did so he chuckled and repeated to himself, "I performed the Ancient Disappearing Trick. I am great after all."

After a while he calmed down and sat at the table again. In front of him he placed one of the books and began leafing through it.

"Now if only I could remember what spell I used. At the time I was in such a state that I said the first thing that came into my head. Now where is it?"

After some time searching through the book, he sat back

with a blissful smile on his face. "I can't find the spell right now. But what does it matter? I did it. Making an elephant disappear is no small trick."

He picked up a pair of scissors and carefully cut out the article about Cato.

CHAPTER 8

CATO FOLLOWS
HIS TRUNK

When Cato woke up that morning, he discovered he was lying on sheets of paper instead of his usual bed of straw. This reminded him that he was not at the circus any more. He remembered a dizzy ride, swinging through the air, then a drink of water and a shower, followed by a meal of soft, thick ropes from a strange tin.

He seemed to be in a big wooden box. In the roof of this box there was a gap through which a shaft of sunlight fell, faintly lighting up everything inside.

As he stretched and lifted his trunk and flapped his ears, he remembered that he was not his usual self—something had made him tiny.

Cato decided to do some exploring—he had never been inside a dresser drawer before. If Sam Fleming had managed to open that drawer, he would have found not only stacks of pencils held together with rubber bands, sheets of white drawing paper, and erasers, but a mouse-sized elephant. He would also have found letters, some opened and some unopened, which had fallen through the hole into the drawer below, just as Cato had done. No doubt Sam may have found a use for these things, but to Cato they were all strange.

I must be comfortable if I'm going to stay here, Cato thought. He began clearing away some of the things. He was used to watching and helping when the circus gear was being packed and unpacked, so he knew how to tidy things up. With his trunk he collected all the pencils and piled them at one end of the drawer. He stacked some of the tracing paper so that it made a soft bed near the front of the drawer.

He also found something else. Scattered throughout the drawer were lots of pieces of coloured paper with pictures and numbers on them. Some were greenish and some were a reddish colour. There were also some attractive blue ones. These he collected and stacked on top of each other in a corner.

After a while he realised that it was breakfast time. Last night, before he had fallen through the hole, he had seen plenty of food.

I've got to get up there somehow, he thought, hungrily.

Getting out might have been easy if Cato had been a monkey that could climb, or a dog that could jump. But for an elephant, unable to do either of these, it was just about impossible. He looked up at the strip of light above him, trying to work out ways of getting up there.

On the floor of the drawer he found a long piece of wood with little black lines and numbers along one side.

If I can't climb, swing or jump, at least I can lift things, thought Cato, and I can walk up sloping boards. So that is exactly what I will do.

Lifting the board with his trunk, he managed to lean it against the edge of the hole above him. Carefully he placed one foot on the board, but it wobbled.

Deciding he needed something to hold it firm, he reached out and pulled two erasers towards him. He jammed these against the end of the board. Then he tested the board again. This time it did not move.

Carefully he took a step forward and upward. He took another step, and then another.

This is great, he thought. Now I can get out and find something to eat. I might even be able to find my way back to the circus.

When he reached the top, he slowly pushed his head through the hole. As he did so, some more of those coloured pieces of paper with printing on them slipped past him and fell into the drawer. Slowly, he looked about.

There was a sudden, loud noise. The back door was pushed open, and in rushed an enormous boy wearing a school uniform and thick spectacles. In his hand he waved a newspaper.

"Just look at this, Sam!" the boy shouted.

Cato quickly pulled his head back into the hole. Although he could not see Sam and John Darcy, he could hear what they were saying. He heard his name. They were talking about him.

"So he hasn't been found yet," he heard Sam say.

Cato wanted to shout, "I'm here. Look over here!" Instead, he stayed on the board in his drawer. Who would believe that a tiny elephant found in a kitchen drawer was the famous Cato, the circus favourite?

Sadly he climbed backwards down the board. He wondered if he would ever get back to the circus, his home. He thought of the sweet smell of hay, the feel of sawdust under his feet, the excitement of being in the ring, the sounds of laughter and music. Would he ever experience them again?

As he reached the bottom of the board, he thought: Anyway I'm glad I'm a circus elephant and not a jungle elephant. Only circus elephants know how to walk on boards and do the things I have learned to do.

He still had not had any breakfast, but he had just discovered something wonderful. He had discovered all the smells of Sam's kitchen. There had been a delightfully mixed aroma of apples, peanuts, bread, strong cheese, soup from a tin, and, just faintly, there lingered a whiff of fish and chips.

Cato sighed. Tonight, when all the humans were asleep, he would climb out again. This time he would make sure he had a real feast.

CHAPTER 9

THIS PLACE IS UNSAFE

Sam was still working at the easel later in the morning when there was a knock at the door.

"Come in!" he shouted impatiently, irritated by the interruption. Whoever was at the door did not come in, but knocked again.

"Botheration!" muttered Sam, and wiped his hands on a piece of rag. He strode over to the door and opened it. A large man dressed in a business suit was standing on the doorstep.

"Mr Fleming?" asked the man.

"Yes, I'm Sam Fleming."

"Brown is my name," the man said, holding out his hand. "I'm from the council. I'm the . . . er . . . building inspector."

Sam shook the man's hand and said, "You'd better come in." He stood back to let Mr Brown walk past.

"You see, . . . Mr Fleming," said Mr Brown, looking around, "you see, this cottage is considered unsafe. It is likely to fall down at any time. It is very unattractive to look at. In fact, it's a disgrace to this area. We have written to you a dozen times about it, but you've never replied. My council has decided that it must come down."

"Is that so?" Sam was so annoyed that his beard shook as he spoke. "Well, for a start, I don't call it a cottage. That's not what it's meant to be. It's a studio."

"Well, whatever it is, Mr Fleming, it is still regarded as unsafe. Surely you would like to live in a more satisfactory home?"

"My studio is entirely satisfactory to me," Sam defended. He began to stride around the studio with Mr Brown following him.

"To begin with, Mr Brown, I designed it so I could have this long window here. It goes along the northern wall, you see. That's to let in plenty of light."

"Yes, well er . . ." began Mr Brown.

"And another thing—my bed is right here, so I am never far from my work. And another thing—the kitchen is small and handy so that I don't have to waste time going a long way to get a bite to eat."

"Yes, impressive, most impressive," muttered Mr Brown, stepping carefully around some spare canvasses stacked on the floor.

"So you see, Mr Brown, this isn't just an ordinary cottage. This is my studio, and it happens to be the only artist's studio in this town."

"Yes, I understand all that." Mr Brown looked around for a place to sit, but all the chairs had things such as brushes and tubes of paint on them, so he stood awkwardly in the middle of the studio. He looked almost as though he was posing for a picture.

"Yes, I understand," he continued, "but the whole trouble is that the building is not safe. It won't be much good as a studio if it all tumbles down around you, will it?"

Sam did not say anything, but he had the unhappy feeling that Mr Brown was right.

"Now my suggestion, Mr Fleming, is this. Build another—er—studio, just as good as this one. It can have a long window and everything else you need. But this time put up a solid building on your own block of land. Get a builder to do it for you. Make it a good strong place that will last. Then my council will be quite happy."

"Jolly good idea," said Sam quietly. "But you've forgotten one thing. I'm an artist, not a millionaire. I haven't got the money to build a place like that."

"Well it was just a suggestion," replied Mr Brown.

"Tell me one thing," Sam continued. "You say I've got to move, and if I don't the council will pull this building, my studio—my home—down. How much time have I got?"

Mr Brown turned a little pink with embarrassment.

"Now Mr Fleming, we are only thinking of your safety. We won't pull it down for another two or three months. I think this cottage will stand for at least three more months, unless we get a hurricane or a cyclone—but that's most unlikely. Yes, you will certainly have three months in which to find other accommodation."

CHAPTER 10

JOHN DARCY'S BRILLIANT IDEA

When John Darcy arrived home from school that afternoon, he saw Sam walking out the side gate.

"I'm just taking a stroll down to the circus," Sam said. "Cato is still missing. I heard about it on the radio. What about coming with me?"

"Right!" answered John Darcy. "I'll just put my school bag inside and tell Mum."

The circus was not the happy place it had been. The performers sat around dejectedly or stood in sad, little groups. No one was practising on the tightrope or the swings. Even the animals looked anxious.

A gloomy and dejected Mr Borrill greeted them at the door of his caravan.

"John Darcy," he said sadly, "and Sam."

"Any news?" Sam asked.

"Nothing," groaned Mr Borrill. His tartan waistcoat

and black trousers were crumpled, and his shoes unpolished. "Nothing," he repeated.

"Did the police find any clues?" asked John Darcy.

"No, they didn't. Cato has disappeared without a trace. A lot of people have come to the circus just out of curiosity. They stand about saying things like, 'It's probably just a publicity stunt'. They say that, but they don't buy tickets for the circus. I tell you, Sam, without Cato I might as well have no circus at all."

Stella came to the caravan door.

"Come on in. Let's have a cup of tea," she said, looking at Sam and John Darcy. She realised that her father needed some company when he was feeling as depressed as this.

The four of them sat around the table in the caravan, drinking tea and munching chocolate biscuits. In no time, Sam found himself telling the Borrills about his own problems.

"Do you mean to say they can put you out of your own home?" asked Stella, shocked.

"Yes, it looks as though they can," Sam replied. "They say it's not safe. I've got three months to find somewhere else to live."

"That's one problem I've never had," said Mr Borrill. "I've always had my caravan. Say, that's an idea, Sam. Why not buy a caravan? It makes a very comfortable home."

"Mr Borrill, I couldn't even buy a toy caravan. Artists don't make a lot of money, you know." Sam dunked his chocolate biscuit. He kept it in his tea so long that the chocolate melted, flavouring it.

"But with your talent . . .," began Stella.

John Darcy spoke up. "Sam does make a lot of money. I

know he does—but he doesn't know how to look after it. For one thing, he gives it away."

"Do you mean he wastes it?" asked Mr Borrill.

"No, it's not wasted," replied John Darcy. "I mean, there was the time I wanted a microscope. Mum couldn't afford to get me one, so Sam bought one for me. Not a cheap one, either. It was a really good one. He sent away to the city for it."

Stella smiled at Sam.

John Darcy continued. "Then there was the time he found out that a boy in my class had never been to the beach. Sam gave the boy's mother a train ticket and arranged for him to stay at a holiday place. Then there was the time . . ."

"Enough!" interrupted Sam. "Not another word." He took a big mouthful of his chocolate-flavoured tea. "Stella, this is the best tea I've ever tasted. Now, let's change the subject. Le Vram, that magician, he was in a thundering rage yesterday after the matinee performance. What's become of him?"

"Huh, Le Vram!" scoffed Mr Borrill contemptuously. "I'll tell you about him." He told of their quarrel, Le Vram's jealousy, and the magician's threat to ruin the circus.

"He's left the circus. He stamped out of my caravan and I haven't seen him since. I've been too concerned about Cato to waste much time thinking about jealous magicians. If he does show up again, I certainly won't employ him. As far as I'm concerned he's finished with the circus for ever."

"I hear they've had a lot of terrible thunderstorms along the highway, and at some little town in the mountains," Stella remarked. Then she looked puzzled and said, "Now why on earth would I say a thing like that, when we weren't even talking about the weather? We were talking about that wicked magician. I tell you, Father, I never liked him very much. I advised you not to hire him in the first place. I thought he looked evil."

When it was time to go, Sam said to Mr Borrill, "I know your elephant will turn up. Elephants never get lost. He's probably gone for a short holiday all by himself. He'll be found. Don't you worry any more. Well, we must be off."

As they walked off through the quiet circus ground, John Darcy felt sad. He wondered if he would ever see the circus people again.

On the way home he was very quiet. Sam spoke to him a couple of times but he did not answer. He was thinking.

When they arrived home, John Darcy found his mother in the kitchen making cakes.

"Well, John," she said as he walked in, "your tea's ready. I've been baking all day. I've made a lot of cakes for the Hospital Aid Society's street stall tomorrow. But I've saved some for you."

John Darcy answered with a vague, "Oh, hello Mum," and walked through the kitchen.

Well, thought Mrs Darcy, he *must* have something on his mind. He normally jumps at a chance to eat cakes.

* * *

After his evening meal at home John Darcy wandered over to the studio. Sam was sitting at a table, sketching, while a plate of stew remained untouched beside him.

John Darcy roamed around the studio for a while looking at Sam's work. His favourite painting was one called, "Trapeze Artists". It showed two trapeze fliers, a man and a woman, performing on a high swing. Actually, the people in the picture were quite small. The tightly-stretched canvas of the big top arched above them. Below them, small and far away, John Darcy could see the crowd—blurred—as the trapeze artists would have seen them if they had glanced down during their dizzy flight. The trapeze fliers looked tiny and alone in that vast space, as though all they had to depend on was each other—which was true. The man had just spun in a somersault and was about to clutch the woman's outstretched hands. The hands, although the person was small, appeared large, strong and dependable.

"Your paintings seem to be alive, Sam," remarked John Darcy after a while. Then he added, "You've got a lot of pictures, haven't you?"

"Hmm," Sam muttered absently.

"There must be dozens."

"Quite a few," Sam replied.

John Darcy walked over to him and clutched his shoulder. "Listen to me, Sam; I've got a brilliant idea."

"What is it?" asked Sam, looking up from his sketching.

John Darcy still clutched Sam's shoulder. "You need money. Right?"

"Right," agreed Sam.

"And you're an artist. Right?"

"Right."

"Well, I know the very way for you to earn money, Sam. Have an exhibition!"

"An exhibition!" Sam repeated.

"Yes—an art exhibition. Put all your paintings on display; invite people to come. They can pay to come in, then they can buy the paintings. That way you'll sell them all, and you'll have enough money then to build yourself a brand new studio. You might even buy a caravan, as Mr Borrill suggested. Isn't that a great idea?''

Sam sprang to his feet. "You're right!'' he cried.

He raced around the studio, picking up paintings and drawings and looking at them.

"Here we are: sad clowns, happy clowns, angry lions, shy lions, brilliant sunsets, stormy skies. Dozens more. Dozens! You're right, John Darcy, that's exactly what I'll do. Let's hold an exhibition. Then I won't have to worry what the council does about this studio.''

CHAPTER 11

IN THE NEWSPAPER AGAIN

"Now, let's do some planning, Sam," said John Darcy one night. It was a week since they had first discussed the exhibition.

"Planning for what?" asked Sam. He was sitting by the long window, looking out across the street. On the opposite side of the street was the picture theatre. A line of people waited at the ticket box.

"For the art exhibition, of course," replied John Darcy in a businesslike way.

"The exhibition. Oh, yes, I remember," said Sam, turning away from the window. "But what could there possibly be to do? All we have to do is hang up the paintings, then tell everyone to come and look at them."

John Darcy sounded exasperated as he spoke. "It's not as easy as that, Sam. I've been talking to Mum. She's organised lots of things like this. You know, she's on the Childrens Home Committee and she's in the Hospital Aid

Society and the Garden Club and the Discussion Group
. . ."

"I know, I know—she's in everything," Sam interrupted. "You're right. If there's anyone who knows about organising things, it's your mum. What does she think we should do first?"

John Darcy explained that they had to hire a hall, have the tickets printed, make posters to put in shop windows, and a dozen other things.

John Darcy suddenly stopped. "Ssh," he whispered. "Sam, I thought I heard something in the kitchen. I bet you've got mice, you know."

"Well, if I have, just leave them alone," said Sam. "The poor things will soon be like me—nowhere to live. Let them enjoy themselves while they've got a home."

* * *

One morning Mrs Darcy bustled into the studio while Sam was working. It was now three weeks since Cato's disappearance. It was also three weeks since John Darcy had suggested the art exhibition. Sam had been working hard at finishing his paintings.

Mrs Darcy, who carried a bundle of letters in one hand and a newspaper in the other, said, "Here's your mail, Sam. I'll put it on the dresser for you."

As she dropped the bundle of letters onto the dresser she spoke again. "Sam, did you know your wallet's here? You're going to lose everything out of it if you leave it lying around like this."

"Don't worry about it," mumbled Sam through the spare brush he held in his mouth.

"Did you hear that the circus has left town?" Mrs Darcy asked, sitting herself on the edge of the table.

Sam took the brush out of his mouth. "Yes, I heard. I hope they come back soon." He thought of Stella as he spoke.

"And that's not all," his sister said. "Here's this morning's paper. What do you think of this piece of news?"

Taking the newspaper, Sam looked at the item that she was pointing to and read it aloud.

Reward for Elephant

So far no trace has been found of Cato, the elephant that disappeared mysteriously from Borrill's Circus while it was in town three weeks ago.

The well-known city businessman, Sir Reginald Bisk, has offered a reward of $1000 to anyone who gives information leading to the finding of Cato.

Sir Reginald reported to be a millionaire, has taken a keen interest in entertainment and circuses over the years. He owns several theatres and has often sponsored special performances. He told newspaper reporters that he hoped the offer of reward money would help to locate the missing elephant . . .

"Sir Reginald Bisk! I've heard of him," exclaimed Sam. "He's the man who arranges Christmas pantomimes every year in the city."

He looked again at the newspaper item. "One thousand dollars. I could do a lot with a thousand dollars. I'd like to be the one to find Cato. It's not only for the money, though. I'd hate to see Mr Borrill and Stella having to close down their circus."

"I think that elephant has been stolen, Sam," said his sister. "I think that someone in this town has that elephant hidden away in their garage."

"Why would anyone want to keep an elephant in a garage?" asked Sam, amazed.

"Well, I've never been able to figure out why people do some of the things they do. That's my opinion anyway. Someone has hidden the elephant away. How on earth they are managing to feed it and keep it hidden, I wouldn't know."

"No, Annie, I disagree. Nobody would be that mean," Sam declared. "Just the same, I wouldn't be surprised if that elephant turned up suddenly one day right here in town."

"Well, I must go now," Mrs Darcy said. "It's the meeting of the Childrens Home Committee today and I think this meeting will be a long one. The Childrens Home badly needs a swimming pool, and we are trying to raise the money to build one. You know how hot it gets here in the summer time. Goodbye Sam."

When she had gone, Sam put down his brushes and thought for a while. He thought about the circus and Stella. He thought about Cato and the thousand dollars. Then he wondered where he was going to live when his studio was pulled down. John Darcy seemed to think that the art exhibition was the answer to all the problems, but Sam thought differently.

It seemed to him that the answer to everything was Cato. He could not work out why, but it seemed to him that if Cato could be found everything would be all right.

* * *

Meanwhile, Le Vram was sitting on the front verandah of his cottage up in the mountains. He was reading the same newspaper item about Sir Reginald Bisk's reward.

He chuckled several times as he read it. "I've really got them baffled this time," he told himself. "That's what magic is all about—baffling. If the audience is not baffled, then the magician isn't any good."

Later that day he cut out the article and carefully pasted it in his scrapbook. He was beginning to gather quite a little collection of reports about Cato's disappearance. From time to time a small item would appear in a newspaper or magazine, and Le Vram intended to keep every one.

He still could not remember the formula he had used to make Cato disappear. Every day he consulted his books of magic or searched through his many notebooks, but, although he found every formula and spell a magician could ever need, none of them seemed to be the correct one. Nevertheless, he knew that, for once, he had performed a spectacular trick.

CHAPTER 12

THE DISCOVERY OF PEANUT BUTTER

When Mrs Darcy dropped the mail onto the dresser, it had woken Cato from his morning nap. He opened his eyes as he heard the 'flop' of the letters falling above him. When one of them dropped through the hole, he placed it on top of the pile of other letters stacked in the corner.

He walked around in his drawer wondering if he had anything to eat, and listening to Mrs Darcy's conversation with Sam.

He felt a little pang when he heard her say that the circus had left town. They've gone—without me, he thought. He wondered if he would ever see the circus again.

Cato was missing the fun of circus life. He longed for the shouts and noise and music and laughter. Most of all, he missed the applause. All his life, people had been clapping and cheering for him—and now there was nobody to do it. In the weeks he had been living in Sam's kitchen, he had learned to do some very clever things, such as: walking along the edge of the kitchen sink; dropping the plug into the hole so that water from the dripping tap would make a pool for him to bathe in; and carrying bundles of food down the sloping board into the drawer.

He felt proud of these things, and every time he did something clever he expected to hear clapping—but he heard nothing. Nobody clapped. Nobody cheered. No children placed their warm, sticky hands on his trunk. Nobody fed him peanuts or buns or apples.

He remembered the time when a little boy had liked him so much that he had tried to persuade his father to buy him and take him home. He remembered the times he had heard Mr Borrill say, "Cato is the star of this show." They were very happy memories.

Sam was reading from a newspaper and Cato heard him say, ". . . offered a reward of one thousand dollars . . ."

One thousand dollars! Cato knew that one thousand dollars must be a large amount of money. Fancy them wanting to pay that much for him—he must be quite valuable.

* * *

That night a bright full moon sent a silvery glow into the little kitchen of Sam's studio. When all was quiet, Cato set out for some more exploring.

The first thing he did was climb down the drainer, slide the plug into its hole and have a bath. He loved water. He loved the refreshing, clean feeling it gave him. He lifted his trunk and let the cool trickles run down his back.

After his bath, he went looking for things to eat. Since he

had come to live in the kitchen drawer, Cato had tasted some interesting new foods. He had nibbled at an apple pie, he had drunk some milk, he had tasted cold coffee, he had eaten cold potato chips and even a whole tomato sandwich.

On the kitchen bench he noticed some things that looked like green trees, cut down and piled on top of each other. Cato broke off one of the leaves and tasted it. They had a crisp, cool, greenish taste. It was celery. With utter enjoyment Cato crunched and munched at the celery. Then he noticed a familiar smell; it reminded him of the circus. He sniffed, lifting his trunk to get the full effect of the aroma. That was it! Peanuts! But where was it coming from? There was not a peanut in sight.

He soon discovered that the smell was coming from an open jar that stood beside the bunch of celery. Hungrily Cato raised his trunk and placed it over the top of the jar, expecting to take out a few peanuts. To his surprise he scooped up a trunkful of buttery substance—but the taste was exactly like peanuts!

What a good meal, he thought, green leaves and peanuts. After a while he felt pleasantly full; so full, that he felt like sending out a great, loud, trumpeting roar. He lifted his trunk, opened his mouth and—squeaked. Yes, it was the silliest, softest, littlest squeak ever made by any circus animal.

I can't even trumpet any more, thought Cato sadly. Nevertheless, nothing could quite take away the good feeling he had after his bath and meal. He broke off a branch of the celery, and, holding it in his trunk like a flag, made his way across the cupboards, carefully stepped through the hole and onto his board, and returned to his home.

CHAPTER 13

THE MEETING OF OLD FRIENDS

Sam soon found out that John Darcy and Mrs Darcy had been right. Holding an art show did require a lot of planning and work.

While Sam was finishing and framing his pictures, John Darcy arranged to have posters made, and went around town asking shopkeepers to place them in their windows. He also arranged to hire the School of Arts hall for the exhibition.

As the day of the show drew closer, the weather grew hotter. The sun stood high in the sky like a red hotplate, and the little town cooked under its heat.

People walked around town mopping their brows and saying, "Looks as though we're in for a hot summer. Very hot."

The footpaths felt hard and dry underfoot. The trees and shrubs growing in the gardens began to droop, and the old people sat on their verandahs in the shade, fanning themselves.

John Darcy arrived home from school and ran into the yard where Sam was making picture frames.

"Guess what!" John Darcy exclaimed. "I've just been down to see about the School of Arts hall. It's definitely vacant on the day we want it, and we can have it."

"Great," said Sam. He was not as excited as John Darcy had expected.

"I thought you'd be jumping for joy, Sam," he said.

"Well, I would be—except that I've just had a visit from our friend, the council man, Mr Brown."

"And what did he want?"

"He came to tell me to move out next month. He said that it's nearly two months since he first came to see me, and I'm still living here. They're going to pull my studio down. I've decided, reluctantly of course, to move into your spare room."

"I see," said John Darcy, thoughtfully.

"Oh, I suppose it's not as bad as all that." Sam brightened up a little as he looked at his picture frames. "Soon I'll have enough money to get another studio. This art exhibition is going to be a big success."

"You bet it is," John Darcy agreed.

Sam gathered up his wood, tacks, saw and hammer. "I've done enough work for today. Let's go down and take another look at that School of Arts hall."

By the time Sam and John Darcy got there the hall was closed, so they walked around outside looking through the windows.

"We'll come down here the day before and hang all the pictures," Sam suggested.

"I've already arranged for that," John Darcy answered proudly. "And I've asked if we can have one of our posters put up outside, on this wall here, so that people walking past will know that the art exhibition is going to be on.''

The sun was sitting on the horizon, looking like a round piece of plastic that had been pasted there. Long shadows stretched across the ground, and the leaves in the trees began to shake and rustle in the cool evening breeze.

"Let's stroll back through town. I want to buy some fish and chips for tea,'' Sam suggested.

Slowly they walked past the shops, stopping to talk to people. Sam knew just about everyone in town. Most people were on their way home from work, and a few were out for an evening walk. Everyone wanted to enjoy the breeze.

By the time they arrived at their own street, it was almost dark. Although the picture theatre was still closed, a few people were gathering outside, waiting for the ticket box to open.

"I wonder what film's on tonight,'' said John Darcy, stopping outside the theatre. As he looked through the glass door, he could see a man inside the theatre—a fat man wearing a tartan waistcoat and a gold watch-chain.

"Sam!'' exclaimed John Darcy. "Sam, there's someone we know in there. Look, it's Mr Borrill.''

At that moment the door flew open, and Mr Borrill rushed out onto the footpath.

"Sam! John Darcy! My old friends. How good to see you.''

He clutched Sam's right hand with his own right hand, and, wanting to shake hands with John Darcy too, grabbed John Darcy's left hand with his left. He stood there like that, shaking their hands and saying, "I've been looking out for you two ever since we came to town. I was wondering when I'd see you."

"What are you doing in town?" asked Sam, still shaking Mr Borrill's hand. "Where's the circus? In the same place again?"

Mr Borrill let go of their hands and said, sadly: "There's no circus now. We've given it up. Nobody would come to the circus, so we sold out and moved here. We are managing this picture theatre now."

"So Stella's here too?" asked Sam.

"My word she is," Mr Borrill replied. "She's here inside the theatre now. She'll be glad to see you two." He turned and stepped inside the doorway, calling, "Stella. Stella, come and see who's here."

Stella opened the glass door and came out.

"Sam, John Darcy—what a surprise," she gasped. She laughed and shook hands with them both. "We've been watching out for you two ever since we came back to town."

"I've already told them that," said Mr Borrill, laughing. "Isn't it good to see old friends?"

More people had gathered outside the theatre. They had formed a line along the footpath and were looking quite impatient. Mr Borrill said, "It looks as though we'll have to open up."

Sam suddenly had a wonderful idea. "Look, Mr Borrill, Stella. I live just across the road. See that building over there, with the long window? That's my studio. Come and visit me tonight after the show. We can have some coffee and a long talk."

"We certainly will," replied Stella.

"Yes, indeed we will," Mr Borrill joined in. "Straight after the show we'll be over."

With a smile, Stella turned and went into the ticket box. She waved to John Darcy and Sam as she started selling tickets.

CHAPTER 14

ANIMAL TRACKS

"I'm having visitors!" cried Sam, rushing into the studio with John Darcy. "I'm having visitors!"

"Calm down, Sam," John Darcy said. "You often have visitors."

"Yes, but these are special." Sam could not calm down. He began rushing around, moving things from one place to another. "I'll have to tidy up. They'll need somewhere to sit. Coffee! I'll make coffee. Have I got any biscuits?"

Methodically, John Darcy went about gathering up the coffee cups. There were two under the bed and two more on the window ledge. Carefully he dodged Sam who dashed around making things worse.

Altogether John Darcy found eight coffee cups. Some still had cold coffee in them and some held paint brushes or drawing charcoal. He took them all into the kitchen, emptied them, and stacked them in the sink.

Meanwhile, Sam tipped up all the chairs, and dumped

everything that had been on them onto the middle of the table. Paper, pencils and paint-splotched ice-cream container lids flew off onto the floor.

In the kitchen John Darcy checked to see whether Sam had enough coffee, sugar and milk.

"You don't seem to have any milk left, Sam," he called, peering into Sam's little refrigerator.

"No milk? I thought I had plenty. What will I do?" Sam called from inside the studio.

"There must be a shop still open, maybe a milk bar," John Darcy suggested.

"Good idea. I'll go out and buy some. Money!" Sam slapped his pockets. "None on me. Where's my wallet?"

He found the wallet in its usual place on the dresser. It lay opened with money spilling out. Sam picked it up and jammed it into his pocket.

"I'll get some biscuits too, and some cheese."

He raced out, banging the door behind him.

When he had gone, John Darcy began to look around for food for supper.

Among the articles on the kitchen bench he found a packet of biscuits. It had been torn open and some of the biscuits had been taken out—but they had not all been eaten. Beside the biscuits, lay a pile of cherries, red and luscious—but only half of each cherry was there.

He found a peanut butter jar on the bench, beside a half-eaten apple. The jar lay on its side with peanut butter spilling out. As John Darcy stood the jar up, he noticed tiny peanut-buttery animal tracks going across the bench.

John Darcy's eyes followed them. He leaned over, close to the bench, peering through his glasses. The tracks went to the end of the bench, then onto the sink. There they were

almost washed away by water. Onward they went, however, across the back of the sink and onto the dresser. By this stage, they had almost disappeared, and only a trace of peanut butter could be seen. John Darcy bent closer. They seemed to go right up to the hole in the top of the dresser.

He moved back to the bench where the tracks were still quite clear. He tried to work out what kind of animal had made them. Although they were not mouse tracks, they certainly had been made by a four-footed creature. He tried to imagine what kind of tiny animal could have got into Sam's kitchen. He thought of possums, lizards, even kittens—but the tracks could not possibly have belonged to any of these.

He went back to the dresser. He heard a faint scuffle, a rustling of paper, inside the drawer. As he had done once before he tried to pull the drawer open, but it was still stuck fast. He leaned closer, trying to look through the hole. It was too dark inside the drawer. He could see nothing.

John Darcy heard a sound at the door, and his mother walked in briskly, carrying a cake.

"I thought I'd find you here," she said, putting the cake down beside the peanut butter jar. "Where's Sam?"

"He's just gone out to buy some milk. He's having visitors tonight after the picture show. Remember Mr Borrill and Stella from the circus? They're living here now, and they're coming for coffee tonight."

"Well, it's a good thing I brought this cake for Sam," Mrs Darcy replied. "It was left over from the Childrens Home cake sale. I thought Sam could use it."

John Darcy told his mother all about how Mr Borrill and Stella had given up the circus and were now managing the picture theatre. While she listened, Mrs Darcy looked around the kitchen.

"He's having visitors you say? Just look at this mess. Half-eaten biscuits, peanut butter spilt everywhere. This will have to be tidied up."

She bustled around putting things away. John Darcy helped, but kept looking back at that closed dresser drawer. Something was there—something was living in that drawer.

CHAPTER 15

IF YE BE ANGRY ENOUGH . . .

"So there is still no clue as to where your elephant is, Mr Borrill?" asked Mrs Darcy.

"No clue. The police have investigated thoroughly. Sir Reginald Bisk has offered a generous reward. We have spent a fortune advertising in all the papers. All to no avail. Cato, the star of our circus, seems to have vanished from the face of the earth."

"It's such a misfortune—and so mysterious." Mrs Darcy sounded very sympathetic.

"The trouble was," continued Mr Borrill, "that I had sent people ahead to all the towns, to paste up Sam's posters announcing that Cato would be performing. He was so popular that everyone wanted to see him. When the circus arrived in town with no Cato, the people called me a fraud. Audiences were so small that I couldn't afford to pay my workers."

"Don't be gloomy any more, Father," said Stella. She was wandering around the studio admiring Sam's pictures.

She walked back over to the chair where her father was sitting. "At least we have friends; and you always did like this little town."

Five people were in Sam's studio: Mrs Darcy was sitting beside Mr Borrill listening to the story of how his circus was lost; Sam was standing beside Stella, showing her his latest paintings and listening to her recount the misfortunes of Borrill's Circus; John Darcy was crouching on the floor near the big window, taking hardly any notice of anyone else in the studio. He was searching through a pile of encyclopedias and other books, and beside him on the floor lay a torch.

"Father, let's forget about circus problems for a while," suggested Stella. "Did you know that Sam is planning an art exhibition?"

"Yes, so I heard. Tell us all about it, Sam."

Sam sat on the floor and stretched his long legs out in front of him. He told Mr Borrill and Stella about the exhibition, and how he planned to make enough money to get a new studio.

"As a matter of fact, Mr Borrill," he went on, "I've thought a lot about your suggestion of buying a caravan. If I could get enough money, that's what I'd like to do. I'd buy a caravan and travel around the country painting landscapes. Out beyond the mountains I believe there's some magnificent country to paint—mysterious light and shade in the mornings, eerie shadows in the evenings . . ."

John Darcy hardly heard the conversation around him. He had found what he wanted in the encyclopedia. He looked up slowly, with his mouth open. He sat for a long time gazing through Sam's long window. Outside, there was darkness with a few pinpoints of light. His finger was still on the open page, at the very place where he had found the information. It was a drawing of the tracks of various jungle animals. John Darcy's finger was pointing to the picture of elephant tracks.

His mind whirred away like a computer. Those round pools of water—they had been animal tracks. And the marks in the peanut butter. He could not believe it! There was no scientific foundation for what he was thinking.

Slowly and quietly, while the others were absorbed in conversation, he stood up and picked up his torch. He slipped out into the kitchen and closed the door behind him.

He looked at the dresser and at the jumble of things on top of it. He stood there absolutely silently for a while, then cautiously crept forward. He switched on the torch, but kept his hand over its light. Slowly he approached the dresser. With a sudden movement he leaned over and shone the torchlight through the hole.

Nothing! There seemed to be some papers there—and something shiny, perhaps a coin—but it was too dark inside, and the hole was too small to make out anything else. A piece of paper could be seen in the dim glow of the torch as he moved it back and forth.

John Darcy switched off the torch and walked thoughtfully back to the studio. Again he sat on the floor with books scattered around him.

". . . very mean of the council, but in a way, I can't help agreeing with them . . ." Mrs Darcy was saying, while Sam poured more coffee.

John Darcy hardly heard or noticed. He was too busy. "If it can't be explained by science, perhaps it can be explained by something else," he said to himself, picking up another book. It was entitled, *Centuries of Sorcery and Magic*—a huge, heavy volume. As John Darcy flipped through it, he saw pictures of witches, hobgoblins, unicorns and creatures with shimmering wings.

The chapters had headings such as: "Alchemy"; "Use of Herbs and Plants"; "Astrology and the Power of the Heavens"; and "Foretelling the Future".

At the beginning of each chapter was a picture. One was of glass bottles and tubes from which there issued coloured vapours; another was of plants in the shape of people; another was of the stars and the moon; and yet another was of a crystal ball.

Nearly every second page showed a picture of ancient documents. They were yellowed and torn, and the writing was barely legible. One told how to create storms at sea, and another told how to turn milk sour "withe no touching by hande".

There were curses: "Howe to make yore enemie's ears turn green."

There were spells: "Place two droppes of this potion into a personne's eyes and he shalle fall in love with whoever he looks upon."

There were recipes: "To mayke warts go away—tayke four toe-nails, whiskers of three rats . . ."

There were chemical formulas: "To mayke pure gold from iron."

Every possible use of magic was listed in the book, but one particular document caught John Darcy's attention. The quaint printing was hard to read, and with some difficulty he made out the words:

TO ALL YE WHO WOULD DO MAGICK

Worke and study well
and ye shall do all manner
of wonders.

Great thinges can be made
small and lyttle thinges
made large, and fair maides
changed into Toades...

if ye be
angry enough.!

"Impossible," John Darcy muttered to himself. And yet—a magician had been very angry, an elephant was a "great thinge", and in Sam's kitchen there was a very "lyttel thinge".

"Impossible," John Darcy said again—but he still wondered.

CHAPTER 16

MEETING A MILLIONAIRE

Many functions, from flower shows to school concerts, had been held in the School of Arts hall, but it had never been busier nor looked brighter than it did on the day of Sam Fleming's art exhibition.

Sam, John Darcy and Stella had planned and organised for weeks. In the final week they decorated the hall and hung the pictures. Every picture was numbered, and John Darcy and Stella had printed lists of the paintings so people would know the title of each one. As well as paintings, there were sketches done with pencil and charcoal, and tiny pictures painted with water colours.

Because the School of Arts was in the main street, people popped in and out all day. Sam wandered around the exhibition, so tall that his bushy beard seemed to float above the heads of the crowd. He talked to people and shook hundreds of hands. Everyone wanted to meet the artist.

It seemed that everyone wanted to buy a Sam Fleming

painting. The headmaster of John Darcy's school bought a landscape to hang in the school assembly hall. The hospital bought a circus painting to hang in the childrens ward. The Childrens Home Commitee did not buy a picture, though. They were saving all their money for the swimming pool.

In the middle of the afternoon, John Darcy was helping Stella count some money when a brisk little man wearing a shabby suit approached him. John Darcy had noticed this man earlier. He had been at the exhibition for an hour or two, and had stood for a long time in front of every picture.

"I'd like to meet the artist," the man announced to John Darcy. "You seem to be organising things here, what about taking me over and introducing me to Sam Fleming?"

"Yes, come with me," replied John Darcy, lifting an eyebrow at Stella.

"Bisk is my name," the man informed him as they walked about looking for Sam.

Eventually John Darcy saw him standing in a corner, talking to a lady who held a notebook in her hand. She was tall and stately, her hair was a startling pink, and she wore sunglasses almost big enough to cover her whole face.

"Hello there, John," said Sam as John Darcy approached with the shabby little man. "This lady is Marjorie, from the local newspaper. She says she is going to write an article about the exhibition for the next issue."

"I certainly am," exclaimed the lady. "This is one of the greatest cultural events this town has ever had. To think that we have a real artist living here in our little town . . ."

"Ahem," coughed the man standing beside John Darcy.

"Oh, yes, er . . .," John Darcy began. "Er Sam, and Marjorie, this is Mr Bisk."

Bisk, thought Sam, Bisk. He had heard that name

somewhere, but could not remember where.

"Sir Reginald Bisk," announced the little man, shaking hands with Sam and bowing to Marjorie.

"Oh, yes!" exclaimed Sam. "Now I remember. Sir Reginald Bisk—you're the man who offered a reward for Cato."

"That's right," said Sir Reginald. He turned to John Darcy. "And are you the artist's brother?"

"No, nephew," John Darcy replied. "Sam is my uncle."

"I dabble in a lot of things, as you probably know," said Sir Reginald to the three of them. "I'm a businessman actually, but I'm interested in many other things. Now—I happen to be opening an art gallery in the city. You know I'm interested in the circus. Most interested. I've just bought some of the pictures for my gallery."

"He looked at *all* the circus pictures," John Darcy informed Sam.

"Yes, indeed I did. They are very fine examples. Now Mr Fleming, I'm interested in your work. Here's my card. I'll be coming to this town from time to time and I'll arrange to see you. I want to see all your work in future because I'm anxious to show it and sell it in the city."

"Yes. Thank you. Thank you," muttered Sam as he took the card.

"Any news of the missing elephant?" John Darcy asked Sir Reginald.

"Nothing positive, just rumours. For example, a farmer fifty kilometres from here rang the police one night and told them to get out to his paddock and bring the reward money because he could see the elephant from his window. When the police got there (without the reward money of course) they found that there was no elephant. The fellow had been looking at one of his own haystacks in the moonlight."

John Darcy and Sam chuckled, and Marjorie poured out a tinkle of laughter.

"Oh yes," continued Sir Reginald, "that elephant has been blamed for just about everything. It's, let me see, nearly three months since he disappeared. If fruit is stolen from trees, the owner thinks Cato did it. If someone a hundred kilometres in the opposite direction hears noises in the night, he telephones the police and reports he's found the missing elephant. By the way, I've met Mr Borrill. Wonderful man. In my opinion circus people bring a great deal of joy and happiness to the world."

Throughout the afternoon and evening, more and more people came to the art exhibition. All of Sam's friends wanted to buy pictures, and people he did not know wanted to meet him because they believed he must be famous. He shook hands so often that he thought his fingers would be too stiff to hold a paint brush ever again.

Late that night the same five people were seated once again in Sam's studio. The heat of the day had been chased away by a cool breeze, and through the studio window the lights of the little town could be seen against the dark sky.

After the excitement and bustle of the day, no one felt very much like talking. They sipped their coffee and offered occasional, sleepy remarks.

Sam murmured, "Every picture was sold. Every one."

"Sir Reginald Bisk doesn't look much like a millionaire," observed Mr Borrill.

Stella said, "He thinks we should get the circus back on the road somehow—with or without Cato."

"By the time we've finished counting the money you

should have enough for that caravan, Sam," John Darcy commented.

Mrs Darcy added, "I think you'll need that caravan soon, Sam. I can feel that wind blowing right through the cracks in those walls."

Sam sat up with a look of surprise. "You know, you're right, Annie. This studio *will* fall down soon. Just look at the cracks in the walls. It's a good thing I'm moving out tomorrow."

Mr Borrill stood up and stifled a yawn. "Do you think we should be going, Stella?"

"Yes, Father," she replied. "It's been a long day. Good night, Sam. We'll come and visit again soon."

"Yes, come on, John—it's time for us to go too," said Mrs Darcy. She and John Darcy stood up and started walking towards the door.

On the way out, John Darcy glanced over at the kitchen dresser. Earlier that day he had placed a lettuce leaf and two peanuts beside the hole. They were gone.

CHAPTER 17

SAM'S BIG DECISION

John Darcy's urgent knocking on the studio door woke Sam the next day. He opened his eyes and blinked at the bright sunlight shining through the window.

"Hold on, hold on. I'm coming!" he shouted, sleepily dragging himself from the bed. He stumbled across the room and opened the door.

"What's all the noise?" he demanded when he saw John Darcy.

"It's nine o'clock," said John Darcy. "You asked me to wake you early this morning, remember? Today is the day when you have to move all your things out. Mum's cleared the spare room. You can't stay in bed."

"It's already too hot to work," moaned Sam.

"I know it is, but Mum's insisting. You have to move today—tomorrow the wreckers are coming."

When they staggered into Mrs Darcy's kitchen carrying loaded, cardboard cartons, they found her taking trays of biscuits out of the oven.

"'Morning," she said grumpily.

It was so unlike Mrs Darcy to be grumpy that Sam stopped and, still balancing the loaded carton, said, "What's up, Annie? Something wrong?"

Mrs Darcy mopped her brow with her apron and replied curtly, "There certainly is something wrong. Our town council makes me mad. Here it is, a sweltering day, and I'm in this hot kitchen making biscuits."

"Well you can't blame the council for the weather, Annie," Sam pointed out.

"No, but it's their fault I'm making biscuits," she snapped.

Sam looked puzzled. She continued: "These biscuits are for sale. The other ladies are making them too. We're going to put them in packets and sell them. They're to raise money for the swimming pool for the Childrens Home."

She put another tray of biscuits into the oven and shut the door.

"That's why this council makes me mad! They should supply a swimming pool. It's ridiculous that in a place that gets as hot as this, there's not even a town pool where people can swim. And look at the way they're turning you out of your home without giving you somewhere else to live. Oh, it makes me cross!"

John Darcy tried to cheer his mother up. "Never mind, Mum. The Childrens Home is sure to get their pool some day. With all the work you and your committee have done, you must have raised a lot of money."

"Yes, 'some day' is right," answered his mother, measuring more flour into her mixing bowl. "A decent swimming pool costs a great deal, and we won't have enough money this year. It looks as though the children will have to wait until next year for their pool."

She cut off a hunk of butter and dropped it into the bowlful of flour. Looking up, she grinned at Sam and John Darcy.

"I'm sorry I sounded so angry. I shouldn't be worrying you two with all this. Here, have some biscuits. They're fresh and hot."

By mid-afternoon, Sam had moved a lot of his things out. The bed, the table and the chairs were still in place, but they were no longer covered with clutter. The studio looked bare and deserted and Sam felt uncomfortable in such a tidy place.

The kitchen had not been touched. The sink, the bench top and the dresser were all as they had been. Sam had decided to move everything out of there last.

As he stood in the middle of the studio looking around sadly, Mr Borrill appeared at the open door.

"Come in," said Sam. Mr Borrill walked in and sat down on Sam's bed. He opened a small suitcase which he had with him.

"Well, here it is. Stella has spent all morning counting your money and sorting it into bundles. Here is all the cash, and here are the cheques. This is a list of the paintings showing how much they were sold for. Stella is very methodical when it comes to business matters."

Sam stared, wide-eyed, at the bundles of money neatly stacked in the suitcase.

"Good heavens, I must be a millionaire!" he exclaimed.

"Not quite," replied Mr Borrill, "but we could say you are a successful artist. With this money you could buy yourself a nice little caravan."

"Just what I've been wanting," Sam said happily.

"The good thing about all this though, Sam, is that Sir Reginald Bisk said he will sell your paintings in his gallery from now on. Sam—you need never be a poor, struggling artist again."

Sam sat down beside Mr Borrill and looked at the money. He had never dreamed that he could earn so much by doing what he loved—painting.

"There's only one place for this," said Mr Borrill, "and that's the bank. I suggest that you put it in the bank straight away."

"Yes, I'll go right away," said Sam, standing up. "You come with me, Mr Borrill. I'll put the money in the bank, and get a cheque book. Then I can get money any time I want, simply by writing out a cheque."

They set off down the street, Sam striding along with his jangly, long-legged walk, and Mr Borrill waddling beside him.

*   *   *

Late that afternoon, Sam hummed happily to himself as he fussed around in the studio kitchen making his evening meal. In his pocket there was a crisp new cheque book and in the bank he now had hundreds and hundreds of dollars. He had only to write out a cheque and he could buy anything he wanted—well, almost anything. He wasn't as rich as Sir Reginald Bisk. He wasn't really rich at all. He was simply an artist who had managed to earn some money at last.

As his sausages sizzled in the pan, he made plans. He would buy a smart caravan. He would take some sketch books, some pencils and charcoal and paints—then off he would go. He would travel around the country seeing things he had never seen before and everywhere he went he would paint and draw. The best plan of all was that he was going to ask Stella to marry him.

He scooped the sausages from the pan and set them on a plate. He made himself a mug of coffee.

It was a warm night. As Sam sipped his coffee he grew warmer. Right now, he thought, it would be pleasant to go for a swim and cool off. Annie was right. It is ridiculous that the town has no swimming pool. He thought of the children at the Childrens Home, and how much they needed a pool of their own.

He stood up and walked over to the window. For a long time he stood there, thinking.

This is probably my last night in this studio, my very own home. It's strange how important it is to have a home. He thought of the children again. Many of them had been homeless at some time in their lives; some of them were without parents.

He thought of Mr Borrill and Stella. Every year they had given the children from the Childrens Home free seats at the circus, but now there was no circus for them to go to.

Sam could see the lights of houses winking and blinking in the night. I'm a good artist, he said to himself. I don't really need to travel around in a caravan. I can stay right here, living in Annie's spare room. I can earn more money with my paintings—Sir Reginald said so.

He went to the kitchen, and searched around till he found a pen. Then he took the new cheque book out of his pocket. He wrote out a cheque to the Childrens Home. It was for all the money he had in his bank account. Across the bottom of the cheque he wrote: "For the swimming pool".

Sam then walked back to the window and stood there for a long time, thinking. He thought about the laughter of children at the circus; of the happiness of children swimming; of Sir Reginald Bisk talking about the joy that circus people bring. He thought about Stella, and knew that she would be proud of what he had done.

He was so engrossed in his thoughts that he did not notice that one of John Darcy's library books, *Centuries of Sorcery and Magic,* was lying open on a chair. If Sam had noticed it, he would have seen that it was open at a page that John Darcy had intended to show him, a picture of an ancient document. Judging by the strange spelling and odd lettering, it was many hundreds of years old. The words which John Darcy had read, but which Sam did not see, were:

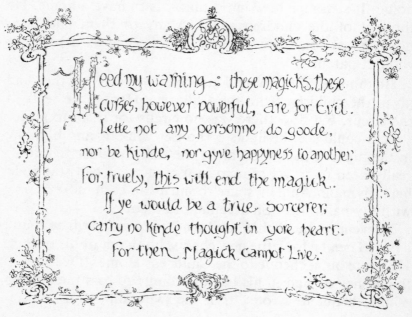

Heed my warning : these magicks, these curses, however powerful, are for Evil. Lette not any personne do goode, nor be kinde, nor gyve happynesse to another: For, truely, this will end the magick.. If ye would be a true sorcerer, carry no kinde thought in yore heart. For then magick cannot Live.

Sam was not aware, either, that in a drawer in his kitchen dresser, a tiny elephant moved—and began to feel uncomfortably cramped in that small space. The elephant stretched in his sleep, gave a contented yawn and, for a moment, felt a strange warm glow.

CHAPTER 18

SAM'S PARTY

The next morning Sam got out of bed early. The sun streaming through the window shone on the peeling paint and cracked walls of his studio.

"Good heavens," he muttered to himself. "It's a wonder this studio has stood for so long. I've always been too busy to notice how bad it was before. Just look at the lean on that wall."

Sam had been told that the wreckers were not coming today, as planned, but tomorrow. He still had some packing to do. His furniture, such as it was, still stood in the studio. His bed and his table and chairs were still there. The little kitchen had not yet been touched.

He stood in the kitchen looking about him. He liked his kitchen. He thought the jumpers and shoes and brushes and papers scattered all over the dresser gave it a cosy look. He felt sad at leaving it. He had to find something to cheer himself up.

Suddenly he had a marvellous idea. He would hold a party—a moving-out party! He would use up all the food and drinks he could find, and he would ask everybody to come.

There were plenty of people he could invite: John Darcy, Annie, Stella and her father; he would even ask Mr Brown, the council man, to show there were no hard feelings—and Marjorie from the newspaper. He wondered whether Sir Reginald Bisk was still in town. Then there were all his other friends, dozens of them. Sam did not even consider whether they could all fit into his studio, he just hoped they could all come.

* * *

He spent the day happily making preparations. John Darcy went with him, all over town, inviting friends to the party. "It's a moving-out party," Sam told them all.

By night-time, everything was ready, and everyone had said they would come. Stella found someone to look after the picture theatre so that she and her father could have the night off.

As John Darcy stood at Sam's sink, washing glasses, he said, "Sam, you're never going to fit everyone in here, in the studio. Where will you put them all?"

"They'll all fit in somehow, don't worry," Sam replied.

Mrs Darcy appeared in the doorway. "Here you are, Sam, I've brought a dozen glasses, in case you need them. Now I want you to come over and see how I've arranged the furniture in your new room."

"All right," agreed Sam. "Come to think of it, I need a bit of a break before anyone gets here. I'll make you a cup of tea, Annie. Come on."

Sam, Mrs Darcy and John Darcy walked out of the kitchen.

CHAPTER 19

DANGER IN THE KITCHEN

Cato had become very clever in the three months he had lived in Sam's kitchen. He had learned how to tip-toe around on the bench, and how to hide behind cups and jugs so that he could hear and see what was happening. Now he was worried. He had heard scraps of conversations and he knew he would not have a home for much longer.

He had seen Mr Borrill and Stella visiting Sam and he had heard them talking about him. He wished he could climb down off the kitchen cupboard, stride out into the studio, and give a loud trumpeting call. He could just imagine how happy Mr Borrill's face would be when he saw his missing elephant. But this was impossible. Cato was only a few centimetres high, and all he could manage was a squeak.

Anyway, elephants cannot climb. Cato was beautifully built for crashing through jungles. He could lift and pull.

He could balance perfectly on tiny stools in the circus ring. He could walk on a board. There were lots of things he *could* do; but no matter what happened he would never be able to climb down from the kitchen cupboard. He could not jump either. When the time came for him to leave, he would have to find some other way of getting down.

Inside Sam's dresser drawer he had made a very comfortable home. His bed of cosily crumpled tracing-paper was in one corner. In another corner, he had a large stack of Sam's unopened mail, which had slipped through the hole. Beside this, he had piles and piles of bits of coloured paper with pictures and numbers on them. Most of them had been in the drawer when he arrived; they had probably been slipping through the hole for years. There were blue pieces, and green pieces, and smaller brown pieces: some of them were crumpled and quite old.

He also had columns of coins which had fallen out of Sam's wallet. Cato had stacked these, and they were just like the stools and drums he had performed on in the circus ring.

Because it was not always safe to be out on the bench top, he also kept a store of food. He had neat piles of celery, biscuits and cherries ready for whenever he needed them.

Yes, life in Sam's kitchen dresser was comfortable enough—but it was always dangerous. Cato was sometimes afraid that if he were discovered, no one would recognise who he really was. John Darcy was forever snooping around, trying to look into the drawer. Cato sometimes had nightmares about being taken into John Darcy's house to be kept in a shoebox—like a mouse or a lizard.

There had been one night, one terrible night, when Cato

thought John Darcy would surely catch him. He had been walking along the top of the dresser and had just reached the side of the sink when he heard him walk into the kitchen. Cato moved as quickly as he could. He scuttled past the jumper, the shoe, the spaghetti tins and the wallet, and reached the hole just in time. He almost slid down the board, and hid behind the stacks of coloured paper.

A bright light appeared above him; when he looked up he was dazzled. Behind the light he had seen two huge circles glinting—John Darcy's glasses.

He overhead Sam planning the party, and knew that by night-time the studio would be packed with people.

Cato was planning what to do. He decided that now, before the party guests started arriving and while Sam and John Darcy were busy, he would slip out, have a bath, and a big drink of water, find some more food, and then come back to the drawer.

Tomorrow he would find a way, some way, of getting out of the kitchen before the building was pulled down. Perhaps he could then live in the wild like a jungle elephant.

He began to walk up the ramp. It would be good to splash around in some cool water, and nibble at some party food before Sam's guests arrived.

Suddenly he felt a bump. His head had hit something. Puzzled, Cato looked up and discovered he had reached the top of the board. He had never hit his head before. He looked up again. Yes, there was the hole; all he had to do was keep walking—but something was stopping him. With dismay, he realised that his head would not fit through the hole.

He tried to pull himself up with his trunk, but it was no use. He just could not get through.

He backed down the ramp and stood at the bottom. He
was so confused. He looked up at the hole and wondered
what had happened. Suddenly he realised: he was growing!
Hooray, he was growing! It must have begun while he slept
the night before. He would soon be his normal size again.
Then he could go back to the circus—to sweet-smelling hay
and sawdust, and cheers and clapping.

But what if he only grew a little bit? What if he only grew
so much that he could never get out of the drawer?

He paced backwards and forwards wondering what to
do.

As he paced, he began to hear voices. It was Sam and
John Darcy coming back with Mrs Darcy. He could picture
exactly how they would look. Sam, long, lean and bushy-

bearded; John Darcy looking knowingly through his heavy spectacles; and Mrs Darcy, cheerful and businesslike. Wouldn't they be surprised if they knew there was an elephant in the kitchen!

He heard more voices as Mr Borrill and Stella arrived. Soon he heard laughter and music, and glasses clinking. The party had started.

CHAPTER 20

THE UNINVITED GUEST

Sam often had parties and visitors, but never before had so many people crammed into the studio. They jostled and bumped each other as they tried to move around. Some people found themselves a comfortable corner and did not bother to move from it. People sat on the bed, on the work bench, on the chairs, on the floor. Sam opened the big window, and people spilled out onto the lawn and even onto the footpath.

They talked, they told jokes, they laughed. They listened to music, they sang and they danced (when they could find room).

When Sam looked around, he wondered if he had really invited so many. He asked John Darcy what he thought.

"Of course you invited them," John Darcy replied, busily opening packets of pretzels. "You went about town saying, 'I'm having a party tonight. Everyone is invited.' That's what you said. You invited nearly the whole town. That didn't surprise me. It's exactly what I expected you to do."

"So I did, so I did," Sam agreed as he swished bottles around in a bucket of ice. "I know so many people—I didn't want to leave anyone out."

Mrs Darcy struggled about amongst the crowd, telling everyone that Sam had given all his money to the Childrens Home for a swimming pool.

She approached Mr Brown, from the council. "Do you know what my brother did? All the money he earned from his art exhibition, the money he worked so hard for, he has given to the Childrens Home."

She told Sir Reginald Bisk, who was talking to Stella.

"That man will never be a millionaire," said Sir Reginald, "but he will always have a million friends."

"I'm not at all surprised," Stella said. "That is just the kind of generous thing Sam *would* do."

Marjorie, from the newspaper, joined in: "That is the most heart-warming story we've had this year. I'm going to write about it in the paper. We might even put it on the front page."

Sam smiled happily as he looked around at all his friends. I'll never get that caravan now, he thought, I might never even have another studio, but who needs those when I have so many friends?

* * *

Inside the drawer, Cato heard the sounds of the party. It seemed that everyone in the world was having a wonderful time—except him. He tried to think of a way to get out of the dresser drawer. The only possible way was to batter down the sides of the drawer. Although the dresser was old and leaned to one side, it was made of very solid timber.

Knocking the sides out would not be easy—it might even be impossible.

He wished that he had started to grow while he was out of the drawer the last time, then he would not have been trapped. I'll try once more, he thought. I'll try to rip some wood off near the hole. Then it might be big enough for me to get through.

He stepped onto his ramp. As he took a few steps upwards, the board began to bend. He went further. Suddenly the board snapped in two—Cato crashed down onto the piles of coloured paper. Coins, paper, cherries, brushes and pencils were scattered about the drawer, and Cato was sprawled amongst them.

* * *

Meanwhile the party continued, as noisy and happy as a carnival. Everyone agreed that it was the best party the town had ever had.

"It looks as though half the town is here tonight," Mrs Darcy said to Mr Borrill.

"Yes, they must be—and the other half is over the road at my picture theatre."

Sam soon decided it was time for supper. He brought out dishes of spaghetti, cold meat and salads, and his friends helped to arrange them on the workbench.

While Mrs Darcy was helping with the food, Mr Brown came up to her. "I have an idea," he said, "You seem to know a lot about committees and things like that."

"Yes, I do, I enjoy organising things," Mrs Darcy answered.

"You should become a member of the town council," Mr Brown suggested.

Mrs Darcy gasped with surprise. "The town council?"

"Yes," said Mr Brown. "This council needs people who are energetic and not afraid of work. We need people who are interested in things that happen here."

"Well, I like the idea," she said.

"There's an election coming up soon. Try to get people to vote for you. Then you can help the town in all sorts of ways."

"I'd like that," replied Mrs Darcy.

There was no more time for conversation as Sam's guests began to crowd around the table for supper.

John Darcy stood at one end of the table with a plate of food in his hand. He was looking puzzled. He kept hearing bumps and bangs in the kitchen. Once, he had gone in there and looked—but he saw nothing unusual, so he came back to the party. He kept hearing it though. Every now and then there would be a bump or a knock.

When everyone was eating, Mr Brown walked to the end of the table and stood up on a chair. He gave a cough and knocked a spoon against a glass several times to attract attention. Everyone turned and looked at him.

"Ladies and gentlemen," he began.

John Darcy heard Sam mutter into his beard, "Oh, no, don't spoil the party with speeches."

"I don't want to bore you all with a speech," continued Mr Brown. "However there is something which I feel you all should know. First, there is an election coming up soon in this town. Mrs Annie Darcy has agreed to stand for council at the next election. As someone who has done so much for this town through her various committees, she will be very good on the council."

Everyone clapped.

"Next, my friends, I want to tell you about a most unselfish act. Our host, Sam Fleming the artist, recently held an exhibition, as you all know. His main purpose was to earn money so that he could buy himself a new home, perhaps a caravan, because unfortunately this studio cannot be allowed to remain here any longer."

Sam began to feel embarrassed. He really had not wanted anyone to know about his gift to the Childrens Home. Slowly, as Mr Brown spoke, Sam moved towards the kitchen door.

"Well," Mr Brown went on, "that art exhibition was an outstanding success. Sam made a lot of money, and he well deserved it. Now, my friends, listen to this. The Childrens Home has had no swimming pool—at least not until now. They are soon to have one, however—Sam has given all his art-exhibition money to the Childrens Home for a pool. Let us all show our appreciation."

There was loud clapping and cheering. Everyone looked around for Sam—but he was not aware of what was going on. He was standing in the kitchen doorway, with his back to the crowd.

As the cheering died down, there was another loud noise. It came from the kitchen. It was a splitting, crunching, cracking noise: sounds of breaking, falling and smashing. The building shook. Suddenly, people stopped talking—certainly no one thought of eating. They looked at each other with alarm.

The splitting and crunching sounds seemed to go on for a long time. Sam stood in the doorway staring into the kitchen; his guests just stared at his back. What, they wondered, was happening.

Finally, there was another noise—a long, loud,

trumpeting sound. It was the trumpeting of an elephant.

Sam turned around, his eyes wide with surprise and his beard shaking.

"You'll never believe this, but there's an elephant in the kitchen."

Mr Borrill ran to Sam's side, shouting, "Cato! It's Cato!"

They all rushed towards the doorway, trying to see into the kitchen.

"Sam!" exclaimed Stella, "Your kitchen is in ruins!"

"Soon the whole building will be in ruins!" shrieked Mrs Darcy. "Everybody run!"

Cracks were opening up in the walls of the studio. The building was so flimsy that there was really no chance that anyone could be hurt. All Sam's guests scrambled out onto the lawn.

At that same time, the picture show across the road had finished, and the theatre crowd was pouring out onto the street. Seeing the excitement at Sam's place, they all streamed across the road and watched.

The empty studio was slowly falling apart. Then, with a final crash, the whole building crumbled and fell to the ground, as though it were made of cardboard. All the time the loud, happy trumpeting of Cato could be heard.

People were everywhere. They were on the lawn, all over the footpath, and on the road. The little studio lay on the ground looking like a heap of scattered matchsticks. In the middle of the wreckage stood Cato, nodding and swaying, with a merry look in his eyes—just as he had done at the circus. He was back to his normal size.

Mr Borrill caught hold of Mrs Darcy's hands and danced round and round. "I'm the happiest man in the world!" he

cried. People were crowding around Cato, patting and stroking him.

Sir Reginald Bisk, Marjorie and Mr Brown were standing close by, amazed at Cato's sudden appearance. The whole crowd buzzed with excitement.

John Darcy walked right around Cato a couple of times, then crouched near Cato's back legs. Cato was standing among Sam's wrecked kitchen furniture; his right back leg was in a broken dresser drawer. John bent down and looked closely. Cato was standing in a drawer full of money!

John Darcy hurried up to Sam, who was standing, looking slightly dazed, next to Stella at the edge of the crowd.

"Sam! Stella!" cried John Darcy. "Come and look at this!" They followed him to Cato's side.

"Just look at this," John Darcy repeated, pointing at the remains of the drawer. "You've been putting your wallet on that old dresser for years, Sam. Your money must have kept falling into this drawer that was stuck closed. Look at it all!"

Sam kneeled down for a closer look. When he saw all the notes and coins he jumped up and flung his arms around Stella.

"I'm rich again!" he cried. "I'm rich. I'm—well, not exactly rich, but—look at all my money. There's enough there to buy—to go to—oh, well, let's get married anyway."

CHAPTER 21

THE MAGICIAN WHO CHANGED HIMSELF

The news travelled faster than the wildest hurricane. Newspapers and radio stations all over the country rushed to tell the amazing story of how Cato had reappeared.

Le Vram, who these days always had breakfast near a sunny window, where he could hear the birds singing, switched on his radio to hear the morning news.

He twiddled the knobs for a few seconds, adjusting the tuning and volume. The news began, and, as he listened, he sat back to enjoy his breakfast.

It was a breakfast that was never eaten. Le Vram sat perfectly still as he heard about the amazing events at Sam Fleming's studio. When the news broadcast was over, he switched to another station and heard it again.

In a daze he turned the radio off. His bacon and eggs grew cold as he sat at the table and thought.

"'Astonishing reappearance—house wrecked—standing

amongst the wreckage of furniture.' I believe I've done it. It wasn't the 'Ancient Disappearing Trick'. That's *nothing* compared to this. What I performed was the 'Spectacular Reducing Event'. It's not a trick nor an illusion—but real. I'm the happiest magician in the world!"

He leapt up and danced around. "If I'm not mistaken, and if I remember rightly, it's on page 777 of *Secrets of the Ancients.*"

He located the yellowed, old volume and lifted it down from the shelf. Flipping through it, he quickly found the page. There it was—all set out: the words, the gestures, the secret thoughts, and—at the end—this message:

"If ye would be evil, and cause sorrow, do this."

His hand trembled as he held the book, and he said: "I should be the happiest magician in the world . . ."

Nobody ever *did* find out where Cato had been for those three months. John Darcy often thought about the strange rustlings and bumpings he had heard in the kitchen, the disappearing food and the footprints. He read *Centuries of Sorcery and Magic* from cover to cover, but the ideas he got were so preposterous that he would not believe them.

Sir Reginald Bisk helped Mr Borrill get the circus back on the road, and Cato is the star again. Borrill's Circus has become the biggest and most successful circus in the country.

Sir Reginald decided that since Cato had been found in Sam's kitchen, Sam was to get the reward money. With this, and the money found in the drawer, Sam had quite a tidy sum. He also found that a lot of the unopened letters in the drawer contained cheques and money. These had been from people to whom he had sold paintings over the years.

Some of the cheques were still new enough to be cashed at the bank.

Sam and Stella got married; they bought a comfortable caravan and now travel with the circus. Stella enjoys being back in her old job. Sam is able to do a lot more circus pictures for Sir Reginald to sell at his gallery in the city.

The Childrens Home got their swimming pool, of course, and Mrs Annie Darcy was elected to the town council. She has helped to make her town a happier and more interesting place in which to live.

Since then, the town has become famous: Marjorie's story of how Cato was found was published in newspapers and magazines all over the world.

* * *

In another town—not far away, up in the mountains—a certain Mr Marvel has become very popular as an entertainer. He is especially in demand at children's parties, and often performs for the sick children in hospitals throughout the area.

Never again did he perform the Spectacular Reducing Event. The formula in the book stated, "If ye would be evil . . .", and Le Vram no longer felt evil.

In his heart, Le Vram believed he really was a great magician because he had worked a rare, ancient magic. He had no need to be jealous any more, so he changed his name, and decided that he should in future make others feel as happy as he did. Every day he makes children laugh and hears applause—just for him. People who had known him in the past would have been astonished at the change.

Every year Borrill's Circus comes back to town for many weeks because so many people want to see the famous elephant. Cato is in the ring, bowing and nodding to the audience at every performance.

Mr Borrill has discovered that many of Cato's tricks have improved, especially the one where he walks on a sloping ramp. As he performs, Cato's eyes twinkle—he is the only one who knows where he spent those missing weeks.